That Makes Me Mad!

Steven Kroll

Illustrated by
Christine Davenier

SEASTAR BOOKS

NEW YORK

For Kathleen —S. K.

**To my wonderful model, Josephine,
and to my parents —C. D.**

Text © 1976, 2002 by Steven Kroll
Illustrations © 2002 by Christine Davenier

Text first published in 1976 by Pantheon Books, a division of Random House, Inc., New York.

All rights reserved. No part of this book may be reproduced or utilized in any form or by any means, electronic or mechanical, including photocopying, recording, or any information storage and retrieval system, without permission in writing from the publisher.

SEASTAR BOOKS
A division of NORTH-SOUTH BOOKS INC.

Published in the United States by SeaStar Books, a division of North-South Books Inc., New York. Published simultaneously in Great Britain, Canada, Australia, and New Zealand by North-South Books, an imprint of Nord-Süd Verlag AG, Gossau Zürich, Switzerland.

Library of Congress Cataloging-in-Publication Data is available.
The artwork for this book was prepared by using watercolor.
Book design by Jennifer Reyes.

ISBN 1-58717-183-X (trade edition)
HC 10 9 8 7 6 5 4 3 2 1
ISBN 1-58717-184-8 (library edition)
LE 10 9 8 7 6 5 4 3 2 1

Printed in Hong Kong

For more information about our books, and the authors and artists who create them, visit our web site:
www.northsouth.com

What makes Nina **mad**?

Lots of things—

little,

ordinary,

everyday

kinds of things.

Maybe just the things that make **you** mad, too . . .

When you tell me I like something you know I don't, **that makes me mad.**

Oh, you're going to love it!

Fish.

What is it?

FISH?

Blech!

I hate fish!

When I try very hard and it doesn't come out right,
that makes me mad.

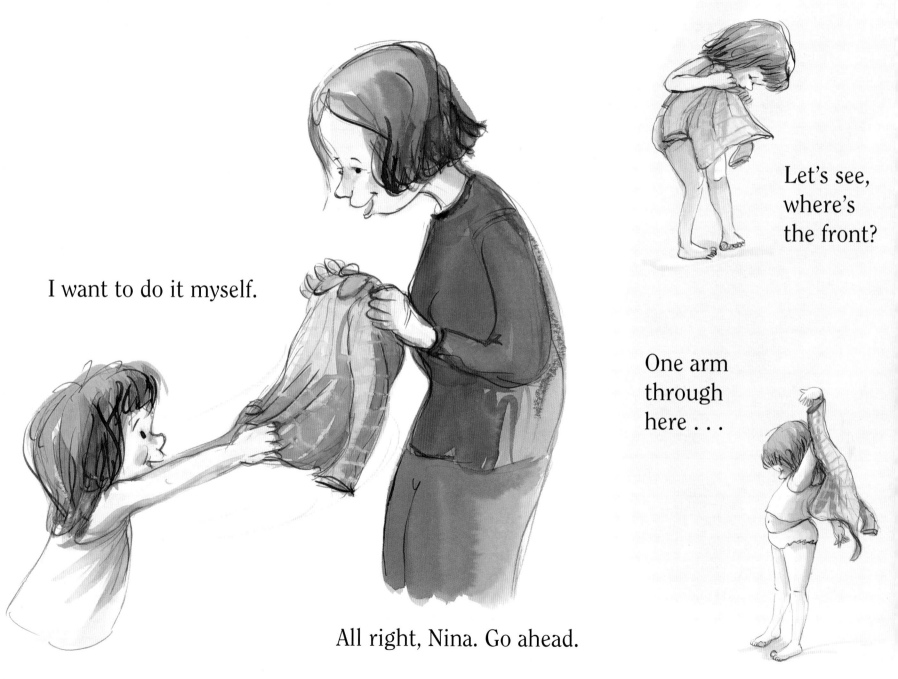

I want to do it myself.

Let's see,
where's
the front?

One arm
through
here . . .

All right, Nina. Go ahead.

When you get mad at me and it's not even my fault,
that makes me mad.

You're in charge, Nina.
I'll be back in a minute.

Cup!   Yes, Tony, cup.

Splash!   Yes, water
splash.

Tony! Stop it.

Cup!
Splash!

Sometimes you talk about me like I'm not even there, and **that makes me mad!**

Look at Nina, isn't she grown up?

And she's such a good helper, too.

Oh yes, she's almost two inches taller and she only had two cavities.

We wouldn't know what to do without her.

It's so nice to see a little girl who knows how to act.

Does she know what she wants to be
when she grows up?
I'll bet she'll be going to school soon.

I'm in
kindergarten!

When I want you fast and it takes you forever, **that makes me mad.**

Hey Mom, look at this.

Just a minute, Nina, I'm on the phone.

When I'm not finished with the best thing I ever made and you clean it up, **that makes me mad.**

Lots of water . . .   some rags . . .   a brush . . .

I know, I need the sponge!

What's all this?
Nina, you sure know how to make a mess!

But that was my car wash!

If I try to cooperate and no one else does,
that makes me mad.

When you make a promise and then you break it,
that makes me mad.

When I need to stay up late and it's always past my bedtime,
that makes me mad.

Time for bed, dear!

Can I stay up and watch *Mooncat*?

No, Nina.

But I want
to see it!

You know you
need your sleep!

But I NEED
to see it!

When it's my turn to talk and nobody will listen,
that makes me mad.

Sometimes I change my mind and it's too late.
That makes me mad.

What'll it be?
The park or the
museum?

I pick the museum.
Will we see the
dinosaur?

Yes.

That dinosaur
is pretty big.

It's very dark in
this museum.

I might get lost.

I hate that
old dinosaur.

I hate
the museum.

I pick the park!
I wanna go to the park!

When I know almost exactly where I put something and it isn't there, that makes me mad.

Hey, where's my bear?
Dad, Tony took my bear!

I don't think
so, Nina.

Yes he did, yes he did!
It's not here!

When you won't let me help and I know I can,
that makes me mad.

But it makes me feel better
when you let me tell you how angry I am!

You're very angry,
aren't you, Nina?

YES! IT'S BROKEN!

It's

Maybe we can fix it . . .
I'll get the glue!

Glue's no good!

See, we fixed it!

ruined!

Mom, I'm glad you're my mom!